# Nicholas Allan

# THE HEFTY FAIRY

RED FOX

A Red Fox Book
Published by Arrow Books Limited
20 Vauxhall Bridge Road, London SW1V 2SA

An imprint of the Random Century Group
London, Melbourne, Sydney, Auckland
Johannesburg and agencies throughout the world

First published by Hutchinson Children's Books 1989
Red Fox edition 1991

Printed and bound in Belgium
by Proost International Book Production

ISBN 0-09-967550-1

Deep in an old hidden wood lay a Fairy Grotto.
In it lived . . .
The Hefty Fairy.

SHE was the saddest fairy alive. Her legs and arms were as thick as mushroom stalks. Her body was the shape of an egg.

  She flew like a balloon and crashed into the other fairies so often they told her she must never fly when they were in the air.

E<small>VERY</small> evening the fairies set off in a cloud of silvery dust, along a candlelit runway and up into the sky. In their hands they carried twenty-pence pieces from the royal treasury, for they were going to collect the milk teeth that children left under their pillows.

THE Hefty Fairy wished she could go too. But the other fairies just laughed at her. 'You're far too fat for such a delicate task,' they said.

So the Hefty Fairy would trot off all by herself to dance round the fairy ring. As she danced she sang the Hefty Fairy Song:

> 'I'm the fairy who's lumpy,
> I'm lumpy, frumpy and dumpy.
> I dance round the ring
> Flapping my wings,
> Going bumpety! Bumpety! Bumpety!'

ONE day the Hefty Fairy discovered The Silvery Thing. She was sitting on a puddle bank wondering if she was really very hefty, when she saw it. She jumped into the puddle and pulled and pulled and pulled. Out it came: a brand new shiny twenty-pence piece! 'Ooo,' cried Hefty.

SHE picked it up and hurried back to her grotto. First she found an oak leaf. Next, she gathered some strong blades of grass and some spider's thread and began to sew. When she'd finished she had a rucksack. She put the twenty-pence piece inside, took a deep breath, spread her wings and fluttered off. She didn't notice the Fairy Queen watching with her royal guard.

OVER the wood flew the Hefty Fairy, across a yellow, a gold and a green field, and then beyond. She had never been beyond Further before, let alone further than Beyond. First she came to a river, then a town. By the time she reached the houses the sun was setting like an apricot on the hill. As night began to fall, a tired Hefty Fairy flew from window to window.

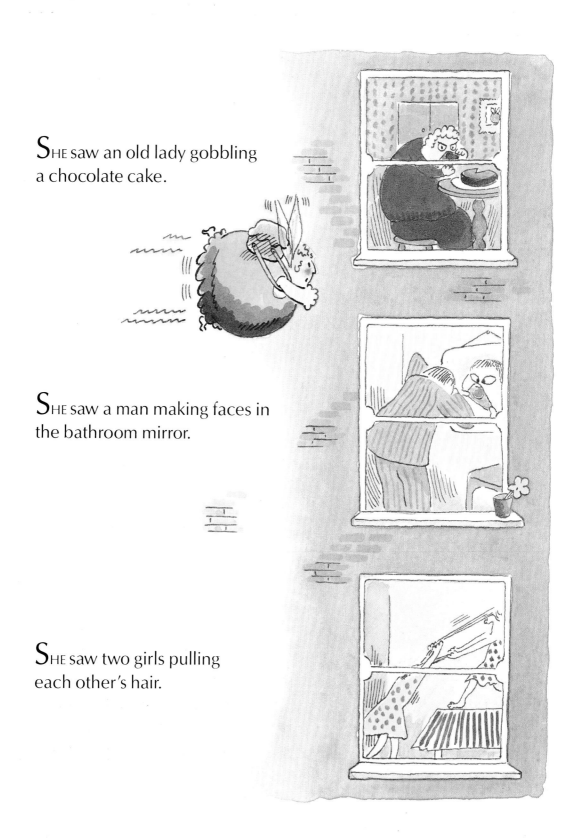

SHE saw an old lady gobbling
a chocolate cake.

SHE saw a man making faces in
the bathroom mirror.

SHE saw two girls pulling
each other's hair.

THEN she saw exactly what she was looking for: a little boy brushing his teeth – and wiggling a tooth with his finger! The Hefty Fairy watched as he went into the bedroom and wiggled his tooth. As he put on his pyjamas he wiggled his tooth. As he said goodnight to his mother he wiggled his tooth. He wiggled it and wiggled it and wiggled it. Finally the tooth dropped out.

'Ooo,' said the Hefty Fairy.

HEFTY knew she had to find the tooth by midnight or the other fairies would collect it first. She waited for the lights to go out, then flew around the house, found a keyhole, and wriggled into it. She pushed and she pulled until she was red in the face. Then she sucked in her tummy and pressed as hard as she could.

Pop! She flew in like a champagne cork and landed on the kitchen floor.

The journey to the bedroom was full of dangers . . .

Hefty was too tired to fly, but she bravely ran all the way down the long hallway and then struggled to the top of the stairs. Slowly and quietly, she crept into the little boy's room.

THE corner of the white sheet was hanging down like a rope.

SHE started to
climb
and
climb
and
climb.
And when she
reached the top
she saw it:
something
oblong;
something
white;
something
glistening;
something that
looked like . . .

A TOOTH!

SHE was far too plump to squeeze through the tunnel made by the pillow but, with a last effort, she flew up and landed on the little boy's nose.

'Atchoo!' he sneezed, and rolled over.

*Now* Hefty could crawl into the tunnel.

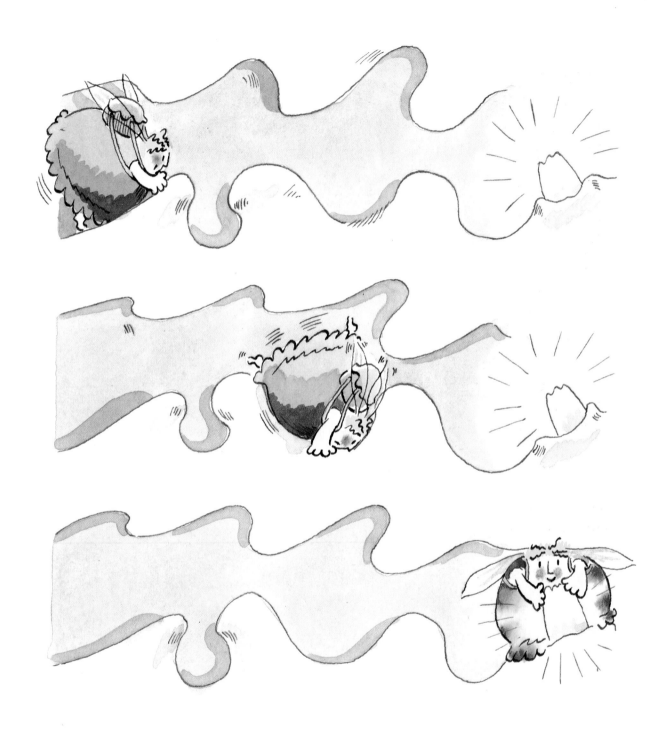

FURTHER and further she went until her fingers touched the
smooth white tooth.

$S$HE grabbed it, left the twenty-pence piece behind, and scurried to the end of the bed. 'Ooo, ooo, ooo,' she cried in a wobbly, worried sort of way. There was no time to lose. Looking down she saw the cat snuggled under the bed.

That's the answer, she thought and, with a great jump, landed right on top of its back. 'Giddy up!' she cried.

THE cat ran through the kitchen, out of the cat flap and into the garden where a triumphant Hefty Fairy bounced on to the grass.

AND not a moment too soon! Looking back she saw the tooth fairies, like two bright stars, by the door. Then there was only a faint silver trail of fairy dust lingering in the keyhole.

It was midnight!

THE Hefty Fairy had had quite enough excitement for one
night. But there was still the long journey home. She felt lonely
as she flew, so she sang to cheer herself up:

> 'I'm the fairy who's lumpy,
> I'm lumpy, frumpy and dumpy.
> I dance round the ring
> Flapping my wings,
> Going bumpety! Bumpety! Bumpety!'

$B$ACK in the grotto the fairies were having breakfast, and
boasting about how many teeth they'd collected when
they suddenly heard a noise above them. Something large and
round was crashing through the trees. Out of the sky dropped
an enormous pink football.

$B$UTTERCUPS and saucers went flying; fairies fell off their chairs. Very slowly the football moved. It rolled one way, then another. A plump foot uncurled, then a short leg, another leg, a wing, two wings, two hands, two arms, and, finally, a dazed head popped out. 'It's Hefty!' cried a fairy. Everyone laughed.

'Yes, it's me,' Hefty said, proudly. 'I've been away to collect a tooth.' She tipped up her rucksack to show her prize . . . but there was nothing there. It must have fallen out! All the fairies laughed. 'You *silly* great Hefty Fairy,' they cried. 'How could *you* ever collect a tooth!'

'I'm *not* a silly Hefty Fairy,' cried Hefty, waving her arms. Tears welled up in her eyes. She picked herself up and started to run. She ran and she ran, through the sunbeams, along the fairy paths, across the fairy ring until she came to the fairy palace.

$S$HE ran through the pearly hall, through the state rooms and
the winter ballroom and into the Fairy Queen's bedroom.
There was the Fairy Queen having breakfast in bed. Hefty put
her arms round her and cried and cried and cried.

THE Fairy Queen loved Hefty very much and felt sad to see her lumpy fairy so upset.

'But it really happened, Your Majesty,' said Hefty. 'I did find a tooth, all by myself.'

'I know,' replied the Fairy Queen.

'You do!' cried Hefty in surprise. Then Hefty remembered that the Fairy Queen knew *everything*.

Next the Fairy Queen did an amazing thing. She stood up and went through a little gold door. When she came out, she was pulling behind her:

> something oblong;
> something white;
> something glistening;
> something that looked like . . .

HEFTY Fairy's tooth!

'OH, thank you, Your Majesty,' cried Hefty, rushing towards the door.

'Where are you going?' said the Queen.

'To show off my tooth,' replied Hefty, excitedly.

The Fairy Queen said nothing. But as Hefty reached the door she stopped and looked round. All at once she remembered how nasty the other fairies had been and wondered if she wanted to show them her tooth at all!

'Of course,' said the Queen, 'the tooth could be a Very Special Secret between ourselves.'

'A completely proper secret?' whispered Hefty.

'One only you and I will know about,' replied the Fairy Queen. And to seal the Very Special Secret she kissed the Hefty Fairy on the cheek.

To share a secret with the Fairy Queen was the biggest honour in the whole fairy kingdom.

Hefty was the happiest fairy alive.

THE Hefty Fairy felt very important. She built a wardrobe and hid her tooth inside. Whenever she felt unhappy, which wasn't very often, she would lift out her tooth and sit in her chair looking at it, remembering her amazing adventure.

She knew then that she was just as good as any other fairy and, somehow, the other fairies seemed to know it too!